Patricia Derrick

Rickity & Snickity
AT THE
BALLOON FIESTA

Illustrator & Composer

J-P Loppo Martinez

Rickity & Snickity

AT THE

BALLOON FIESTA

Every year in Oc-to-ber
Park Rangers pack the van.
Leave the Rocky Mountains
See hot air balloons, first hand.

It's off to Al-bu-quer-que
To the "Ball-oon Fi-es-ta,"
But in the back of the van
Are cubs taking, a "si-es-ta."

Rickity and Snickity
Take a morning nap,
But the cubs hiding in the van
Was not the Rangers' plan.

**Rickity and Snickity,
Rocky Mountain Cubs,
You are the bear cubs
That everyone loves!**

Rocky Mountain Cubs
Around the park they roam.
A big pile of trash becomes
A tem-por-ar-y home.

So many Balloons
On "Ball-oon Glow" night
That when Bal-loons were fired up
The night became "daylight."

So many balloon shapes
Lit up the night.
A cow, a pig, a duck,
Smokey the Bear, all in flight.

Rickity and Snickity,
Rocky Mountain Cubs,
You are the bear cubs
That everyone loves!

Next morning, cubs climbed
Into the balloon.
Cubs were flying in the sky
With balloons passing by.

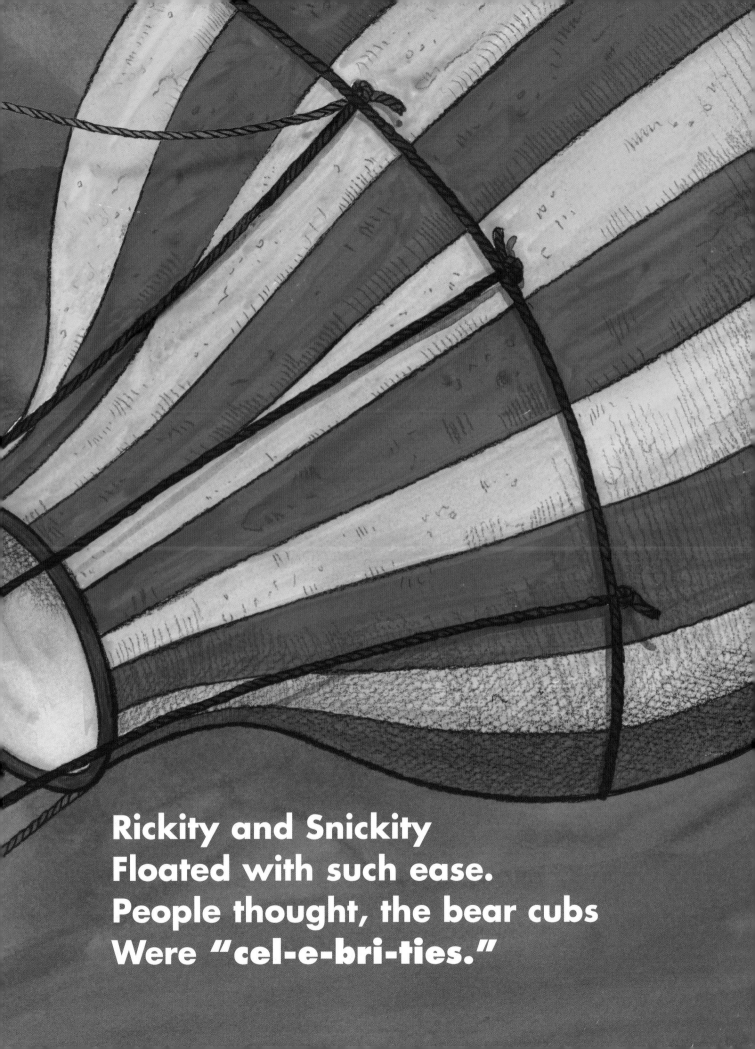

Rickity and Snickity
Floated with such ease.
People thought, the bear cubs
Were "cel-e-bri-ties."

News of Rocky Mountain Cubs
Through Fi-es-ta spread;
In the morning paper, news
Of cubs is what they read.

Rickity and Snickity,
Rocky Mountain Cubs,
You are the bear cubs
That everyone loves!

Rangers soon found those cubs.
Took them to their home.
Back to the Rockies, so
The cubs again, could roam.

The Balloon Fi-es-ta
Will come again next year.
Rocky Mountain cubs say,
They plan on being there.

Rickity and Snickity,
Rocky Mountain Cubs,
You are the bear cubs
That everyone loves!

Rickity & Snickity at the Balloon Fiesta

Lyrics Patricia Derrick - Music J-P Loppo Martinez

Orin the Owl has wisdom for you

Three R's Before Reading:
Rhythm, Rhyme, Repetition
and
"The Neuron Effect"
"Get Those Neurons Firing"

Rhythm, rhyme and repetition are needed before children learn how to read.
These three R's provide patterns and sequences that are found in spoken and written language.

While rhythm and rhyme provide the patterns and sequences, repetition reinforces them.

Each Animalations book has a refrain that children can repeat.
Children love to participate. As they participate in dancing, clapping, singing, they are also learning critical skills that will be needed as they learn to read. Animalations.com will provide further information.

Music and language are interconnected. While music is a great way to introduce new words, it can also contribute to children's learning in many different areas: self-expression, cooperative play, creativity, emotional well being. Furthermore, music and language enhance social, cognitive learning, communication and motor skills.

Rickity and Snickity at the Balloon Fiesta provides opportunities for learning experiences beyond listening to a story. Adapt the suggested activities on this page to provide age appropriate learning for all children participating in Rickity and Snickity at the Balloon Fiesta.

Music and Movement :

Explain the southwestern style of music represented in Rickity and Snickity at the Balloon Fiesta. Explain and demonstrate "Salsa" dancing or bring in a Salsa dance expert to demonstrate for the children. Use native Mexican costumes.

Give children an opportunity to express themselves through movement as they listen to Rickity and Snickity at the Balloon Fiesta. Children's dancing will soon flow in their own "Salsa" style.

Social:

Provide an opportunity for the children to prepare a Mexican Fiesta. Invite parents to provide Mexican clothes for the children. Clothes may include full skirts, white frilly blouses for the girls and vests, sombreros, and western boots for the boys.

Go to the local library and research Mexican music and culture. While at the library, be sure to research hot air balloon gatherings. Help the children find hot air balloons with many different shapes.

Don't forget to research bear cubs while at the library. This is an excellent opportunity for children to learn about bears that live in the Rocky Mountain region. Discuss the fun of pretending that bear cubs can ride in hot air balloons.

Art:

Provide an opportunity for children to draw their own interpretation of the bear cubs riding in hot air balloons. While the children are drawing, they can imagine other animals riding in hot air balloons and draw them also.

Language:

Allow the children an opportunity to explain their drawing to others in the group. Self esteem will "sizzle" as children share their work with others. Invite children to read their work to family members, friends, and grandparents, as well as post their drawings on home refrigerators to share with others over and over.

Search:

Find the duck in the story and count how many times he appears. Act out the duck's antics in the story.

Bear cubs are born in the winter in the mother bear's den. Female bears usually have between one and three cubs at a time. When cubs are born, they are usually the size of a human hand. They keep safe and warm in their mother bear's den. Drinking their mother's milk helps the bear cubs grow quickly. When the bear cubs are about three months old, they go outside the den and start looking for their own food.

Cubs live with their mother until they are two to three years old. By this time, they have learned what to eat and how to find food on their own. At two or three, they go off to find their own new homes. When they are four to seven years old, they are ready to have cubs of their own.

Bear cubs live in forests, swamps and wooded mountains. They eat vegetables, fruit, and meat. During autumn, they eat more than usual to gain body fat to last through their winter "hibernation."

Dedicated to all the children in Albuquerque New Mexico and to those who travel to Albuquerque each year to attend the International Balloon Fiesta.

Patricia Derrick, Author

Master of Education from the University of Utah
Early Childhood and Elementary School Educator
Owner and Operator of Early Learning Schools: 30 years
Assistant Professor, Metropolitan State College, Mesa College Campus, GJ Colorado

Author Patricia Derrick is available for speaking engagements and conferences
Email: info@animalations.com for more information

Dedicated To Fabrice, Stephanie and Enzo

Jean-Paul Loppo Martinez

Born in Brittany France, featured artist, Andre Agassi Charitable Foundation
Worked with legendary artists: Picasso, Miro, Tapies, Adami, Max Pappart
In 2004, his painting Lady Liberty was placed in the White House
Paintings in more than 100 exhibitions, 120 musical compositions in his career
loppomartinez.com

Rickity and Snickity at the Balloon Fiesta

Publishing
4186 Melodia Songo Court
Las Vegas, Nevada 89135

ISBN 10#   1-933818-11-5
ISBN 13#   978-1-933818-11-5

Author copyright 2007 Patricia Derrick
Illustrations and Music copyright 2007 Animalations

Book Designer: William Garbacz

Printed in Korea

Complimentary replacement CD's for libraries:
Send requests to: info@animalations.com

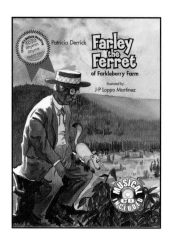

Farley the Ferret of Farkleberry Farm:
Farley and the farmer take bread and jam to the fair, but when the drought hit Foley County, there was no jam to share. Children danced around the vines and made silent wishes in their minds. Find out what happened to the berries on Farkleberry Farm. Message: Farley and the children found a way to help others.

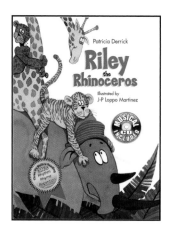

Riley the Rhinoceros:
Riley is called the jungle bus because he gives rides to baby animals as they find their way back home. But, he can't give rides to all the animals because that would be preposterous. Message: ...helping others and friendship.

Dody the Dog has a Rainbow:
Dody the dog is lost and travels through the town and countryside looking for his home. Dody eventually finds his rainbow to help him find his way. Message: There is hope inside your rainbow.

Forthcoming Books from Animalations:
Mr. Walrus and the Old School Bus
Montgomery the Moose
Sly the Dragonfly
Rathbone the Rat